BLOO~~D~~

~~CURSE~~

Don't be alone in the fitting room… Urban legend in Asia comes to life…

Arthur Crandon

Arthur Crandon Publishing

Hong Kong

Arthur Crandon Publishing
22nd Floor, Hing Bong Commercial Building,
Wanchai, Hong Kong.
www.arthurcrandon.com

Publisher's Note: This is a work of fiction. Names, characters, places, and incidents are a product of the author's imagination. Locales and public names are sometimes used for atmospheric purposes. Any resemblance to actual people, living or dead, or to businesses, companies, events, institutions, or locales is completely coincidental.

Book Layout © 2019 BookDesignTemplates.com

Bloodline Curse/Arthur Crandon -- 1st ed.
ISBN: 978-1-9161408-1-3

DEDICATION

This book is typical of the rumors, tales and legends that abound in the magical islands of the Philippines. The Mall Snake Monster is widely believed to have inhabited the basement in a Robinsons Mall, from where it preyed on innocent girls. Most Philippinos know of this tale, and more than a few believe it to be true.

I dedicate this book to my wife, Lynnie Requilme Ceniza, and our wonderful son, Cameron. Lynnie has been a source of inspiration and support in this book, as in my previous works.
Cameron, not so much. But perhaps I'm expecting too much from him. I will expect more from him after his second birthday.

Books are a uniquely portable magic.
Monsters are real, and ghosts are real too. They live inside us, and sometimes, they win.
Either get busy living or get busy dying.

—STEPHEN KING

CONTENTS

CHAPTER ONE

INVASION

Frightened natives cowered in their wooden homes as the fiery torches of the Spanish Galleons lit the midnight sky. Raucous cheering from the close-armed men aboard the ships gave the scene a carnival atmosphere.

Ten large vessels proceeded up the Cebu Straights towards the defenseless town. As they came within range, the deck cannons thundered into life. Flaming balls cascaded down upon the taller buildings in the township center. As they got closer, skilled bowmen picked off unwary townsfolk too slow to take shelter.

Cheers resounded onboard as the invaders watched helpless locals run away and scamper up the nearby hillsides into the forests for safety.

The town was gripped with panic as the first ships reached the deserted moorings and berthed in the darkened and abandoned harbor. There were no troops to greet them, no defenders.

The Spanish had been coming here for years to trade, they seemed friendly. But their military superiority had always been clear. They made it known they'd get what they want by commerce, or by any other means.

They arrived in the dead of night and unleashed a terrifying attack, quelling any notion of resistance the residents may have had. This time they'd come to stay and brought with them an army. Armored conquistadors came with weapons the like of which the locals had never seen before, and priests to make the islanders worship just the one God, their God, instead of many.

There was no-one to oppose the triumphant troops as they passed by the beaches and towering coconut trees that lined the shore, and marched into the Town.

The invaders set up the first Spanish Administration under the Governorship of the Spanish nobleman, Lopez de Legaspi, who grew confident and greedy. Until the Spaniards arrived the island's population had never been invaded or conquered, the people were meek and docile, and very unprepared.

***

Over the following months townsmen and boys built churches, supervised by their new masters, who forcibly converted the people to the Catholic faith. These changes didn't go smoothly. They had scant choice but to comply, but the undercurrent of resentment became stronger over time.

"How long shall we let these invading bullies take everything we have?"

The imposing leader spoke to his council, the forty men who formerly ran his kingdom.

Rajah Tupas used to be the King of Cebu. He'd moved himself and his household to the safety of his hometown inland when the Spaniards landed. The former Ruler had seen his estates seized and his workers forced to work for the Spanish. Local women were taken as brides and concubines for the soldiers, and now the ultimate insult. The Governor had relayed word that his guards were coming to collect taxes and tribute from the Rajah.

Tupas was patient, not hot-headed like some of his followers. The enemy were properly trained, and much better equipped than his ragtag gang. They must plan any action carefully, and he had to have his people onside.

This matter divided his council into two camps. The older men were wary, and terrified of the Spanish. The younger ones felt differently; they were more hotheaded.

They met in Tupas's large home. A cooking pot boiled in the middle of the room, smoke from the wood fire rose and disappeared out of the hole in the roof. His wife cooked chicken stew. He wanted his people there; they'd come if they got food.

"If we give them a bloody nose at least they'll deal with us with respect. If we stand up to them other islands will send fighters to support us; let's show them we won't be treated like slaves."

The men nodded; their bravado fueled by Tupas's growing passion. They'd talked of insurrection for a few months now. He commanded more than a hundred loyal warriors, but he needed more. Tonight, he would tell them his plan; it might bring him more support.

"I realize this is dangerous. Many of us will suffer. Some may die, but we've given up so much. What are we left with? Nothing we used to own is ours anymore. What will we pass to our children?" He paused for his words to sink in.

"If the other islanders rally to us to challenge the invaders we might prevail. We'd give them such a bloody nose they may treat us with more respect." He noticed many nodding heads, but the eldest man, on his right, spoke first.

"What shall we do? They're everywhere, and well-armed. Our men are in the villages, it will take a while to get them here. If the Spaniards see us meeting together they'll suspect we're planning something."

"They won't think anything if we're gathering to go to church. That's something we do all the time. That building is their pride and joy – and it's made of wood. They'd never believe we'd do such a thing." Tupas said.

Most of the men looked puzzled, then one of the younger men understood what their leader meant.

"You want to burn the Church?" The Rajah looked hard at him.

"Is there a better way to show our objection at being forced to worship their god? I've given it a lot of thought. If we concentrate our people in one place, we can overcome their guards.

It'll be night, they won't be expecting trouble. There will be confusion, we should be able to escape. The other islands will hear of what we've done and will support us. It'll be the start of our uprising. We owe this to future generations, to take back our lands."

Tupas has carefully prepared his words for that evening. They were well received.

***

The group started to make plans. Pledges of aid and support came in from the villages. The elders left to prepare for the reprisals they feared might come from such actions, but secretly wishing them well, and hoping they'd succeed. The younger men left for home to spread the story and gather more support.

The attack was set for the following night. If they waited longer, news of their plans may leak out. They would strike at three a.m. During the next afternoon men made their way towards the town square.

The new church stood majestically in the center, a showpiece for the ambitious Spanish Governor. He'd taken a hundred workers from Spain and Mexico for the job and used his own money on the project.

The striking red brick edifice stood out among the simple one-room homes, made with little more than reeds and mud.

Willing warriors slowly arrived from mountains on foot and in groups. Some had wagons full of hay. The straw bundles hid the spears, swords and daggers they'd need later. None of the occupiers suspected what would take place that night. The guards were relaxed and did not inspect the carts. There had been no real problems for a long time, security was very lax.

The insurgents hid and rested in the homes of sympathetic locals close to the church until the appointed time. The Rajah had an elite group of twenty of the best warriors at his house. Ten of them would each take charge of a group of fighters to carry out attacks on different parts of the building. Tupas would lead a few men into the main chapel to destroy the altar with its trappings and decorations.

He dispatched a runner to other houses to find how many men he had. More than one hundred and ninety were ready to fight alongside him. It was enough to keep the guards busy and allow other groups to carry out their mission.

The warriors would all attack at the same moment, otherwise the soldiers may pick them off one by one. During the evening they arrived a few at a time so as not to arouse suspicion. Quietly, they retrieved their arms from the carts, and planned for the fray.

Tupas had concealed a musket, the only firearm they possessed between them, under his bed. He would fire into the air at three a.m. It was the sign, the start of the fight back. The worm was about to turn. For the rest of the day they bided their time talking of tactics, and how they would celebrate afterwards.

"Come on, men. It's time." He said, as he headed his men into his courtyard.

The thunderous sound of the musket shot split the night air. The thirty Spanish troops guarding the church were startled, not sure what was happening. Many of them asleep at their posts, playing cards, or in one case fornicating with a young local girl in the quiet vestry.

Tupas led his band towards the side entrance of the main halls. They usually left the doors unlocked at night. As they neared, shouts came from other areas. Other groups close by were already engaged with guards. He heard the second musket shot and prayed the bullet had missed.

Four soldiers stood in front of the narrow gates. They rose and drew their swords as the men confronted them. One of the Rajah's men ran towards the guards with his pikestaff, striking a glancing blow, but he did little damage except to knock the man off his feet. The guard at his side used the opportunity to thrust his short sword into the man's side before he was could prepare for a second try, spilling the first blood of the night.

Tupas fired his musket for the second time. His aim was true. The ball pierced the thin armor and embedded itself in the chest of the guard. His heart burst and he crumpled. Two men remained on their feet at the door, standing over their fallen companions.

"Help us. We're under attack." They shouted.

The shouts went unanswered; their comrades were busy elsewhere. Tupas's men rushed forward and overpowered the hapless guards. Their leader strode through the open door and into the quiet chapel.

Four of his men carried oil with them. Quickly, they sprinkled it around, splashing the wooden altars, the statues, the ornate drapes and the pews.

"Ok, lads. Get out now, I'll start the burning, I want you all well away from here when the building goes up."

Shouts and cries came from many directions, and no guards were to be seen; his small army was effective.

Tupas stood alone in the large hall. He lit his first torch with his tinderbox and touched the oily floor. The Rajah stood back as blue-tinged flames shot off in several directions.

In the heart of the hall was a centerpiece, a tall and imposing statue of the virgin Mary. It's vivid paint peeled as the flames lapped at the foot and crept upwards.

"It's sacrilege. What are you doing? How can you do this?"

The hysterical voice came from a young priest, emerging from the vestry, wide eyed and incredulous. He paused for a moment staring open-mouthed at the large man. Tupas towered over him, holding a pail of oil in one hand and a flaming torch in the other.

The youthful priest cried out and rushed straight at him. Tupas backed away but stumbled, and accidently splashed oil over the man.

"Father, you're covered in oil, you should get out before you catch light. I've no wish to harm you."

The wide-eyed young man was oblivious to the liquid now seeping into his robes and running down his arms. He struck blow after blow at the Rajah. Instinctively the big man brought his hands up to fend him off. The burning torch connected with the priest's clothes and sparks shot up to his shoulders.

The surprised priest stepped back and slipped on the oil. Flames spread over the rest of his body now. He looked up at the big man in fear.

"Help me, please."

The Rajah pulled away as the young man clutched at his sleeves. Fire engulfed the unfortunate priest. The Rajah could only watch as the flesh on the mans exposed legs melted and burned like candle wax.

"Argh. Please. Why would you do this? What have I done to you? Are you the devil?"

The young priest melted away as the flames spread. Fire was spreading along the reed floor coverings now.

"Curse you a thousand times. You're the most evil man on this earth. How can you just watch? God will damn you for this. I curse your family through a thousand generations. The souls of your descendants will know no rest. Your wickedness…"

The young man could speak no more, his mouth gaped wider as the lips burned away to show his teeth and gums.

With the curse reverberating in his ears and the blood-curdling screams of the dying man echoing around the church, Tupas left the horrid spectacle. The whole town was awake and filling the streets now. Everyone saw the Rajah and his men leave the building as flames shot from the windows and walls collapsed. Bloody bodies of guards and townsfolk lay in the streets including women and children. Guards called to the scene were not too fussy who they killed that night, there was so much anger at the desecration of their church.

With sparks and flames rising high into the night sky from the once magnificent church, their job was complete. Tupas and eight of his men made it back to his house, but one was badly injured with a deep cut to the chest.

"We have to get him a doctor." Said Tupas wife. The Rajah looked at the bleeding man, and realized there was no way to help him now.

"Are you crazy?" One of his men spoke.

"There'll be men here to kill you within the hour – we have to go. Let's get back to our village, maybe we'll be protected there for a while." Tupas shook his head.

"We won't be safe there. They'll come before dawn looking for me. We'll get the family to the hills and hide out. Let's hope our cousins from the other islands come to help us. We'll know soon enough. Come on, we have to leave now."

Tupas looked at his old friend, blood pumping copiously from the gaping wound. The heart was damaged. He put his arm on the man's shoulder.

"Don't worry, old friend, we'll look after you."

The old man smiled as their eyes met. He gasped as the knife entered his injured chest, opening the ribcage and ending his painful life.

Tupas, his wife and children, and a few faithful followers left their compound under the cover of darkness and the confusion. Within hours they made camp in a wooded canyon deep in the jungle. The Spanish were still not familiar with the mountainous territory. The Rajah's family would be safe for a while.

CHAPTER TWO

THE BIRTH

As they were hidden in the dense bush, they had no contact with the outside for three days. On the fourth day Tupas and his wife risked a trip to the village. They blended into the bushes and trees on the road, staying alert for patrols.

The settlement nestled in a canyon between two large mountain ranges. It was secluded and could only be approached by long and winding roads. Only when they approached did they realize something was amiss. The smell of charred wood and burnt flesh filled their nostrils. They hurried closer. The sight that greeted them was so horrific that Tupas's wife was violently sick.

The Rajah scanned around, all the villagers were dead or gone. Maybe some had escaped into the forests, but he doubted it; they would have come back by now. The aggressors left a long time ago. None of the smaller huts were left standing.

The glowing embers of the huts, the animal pens, even the little community house was all that remained. Bodies lay everywhere, women, children, babies, no-one was spared.

The Rajah fell to his knees and wept. His family, his friends, they were all gone. Seeing his anguish, his wife gently gripped his shoulder.

"This isn't your fault, my dear. The Spanish are to blame, not you. Their bloodlust will cost them, they didn't have to do this."

She raised her distraught husband up and drew him away from the smoldering remnants and back into the forest.

"We're not safe here, dear. They won't rest until they've caught you. They'll want to make an example of you. There is nothing here for us now. We must go, tonight. My people are on the coast. They'll give us a boat, but we have to leave as soon as the light fades."

With the practical strength and determination that only a wife and mother can offer, she brought him, still tearful, up the ridge to prepare for their journey.

By night fall they reached the coast and were saying goodbye to their colleagues and family.

"This isn't the end. We won't let those Spanish bastards get away with it. We'll be back, with enough men to finish their murdering lives." Tupas tried to reassure his people, but they could see he was a spent force.

He had no fight left in him now, neither did his people. He left the isle defeated, and with the curse of the priest ringing in his ears. He'd asked for forgiveness every day since the attack, but he sensed that God was not listening.

The Rajah was, at heart, a man of faith, and priests were powerful people, even inexperienced ones. He'd never meant to hurt a priest. He feared this curse more than the Spanish soldiers who at this moment were combing the dense forests, searching for him.

The waters gently lapped at the bank as the leaky fishing boat reached the golden shores of Cagayan d'Oro just before dawn. Tupas had friends and people there who made him welcome and kept his presence secret.

The Spanish Governor sent expeditions to the island to look for him, but they only made half-hearted attempts. They didn't care if they discovered him now. The sacking of his village was punishment enough, it sent a powerful message.

***

Revenge for the burning of the church had been savage. The frightened natives were cowed now, there had been no unrest for months. Tupas and his family made their new life in Cagayan d'Oro, and changed their name to Constantino.

Many locals had married with Spaniards or sought to ingratiate themselves with their masters and adopted Spanish names.

Within a year of the move Tupas's wife was expecting their second child. Their son, Oliver, was sixteen years old.

Maria was a born organizer. She and her maid prepared everything in the home for the birth, but she had to take to her bed before the baby was due. She was very large, and very weak. Everyone was glad when finally the day came.

"I think it will be today, sir. It's going to be a big baby." The old village midwife was bustling around preparing water, sheets, towels, etc.

"I believe she will give birth soon, sir. Your wife is terribly weak. She can't stand much more."

The Rajah nodded. He'd watched her grow weaker over the last few days. He'd insisted she stay in her bed a while ago, but even with rest she wasn't improving.

There was a scream from the bed. The midwife rushed to her.

"Come on, dear, move now, you're dilated. Breathe and push, it'll come now."

The shouts and low groans continued for a while; Maria's face grew waxy. The sweat dripped from her cheeks, dampening the clothes and bed sheets. And then the baby came. A final groan heralded the slow, but smooth, delivery. The midwife took the child and cut the cord. She held it up to clear the airways and start the breathing, sighing with relief when the first gasp for air and quiet cry came from the baby girl. Her happiness was short-lived. Tupas stood by the bed holding his wife's hand. He called urgently to the nurse.

"Come quickly, something's wrong, look." He gestured at his wife's body. Maria was semi-conscious now, but her belly started moving; undulating and rippling as if there was still something inside. Maria woke and looked down. She shrieked again and clutched her husband's hand.

"I've seen nothing like this before. Let me examine her." The nurse inserted two fingers into Maria. It was the nurses turn to shout, and her piercing shriek was ten times as strong as Maria's now pitiful wails. She snatched her hand away. The tip of her middle finger was hanging off, bleeding. The bone was broken and the tip was attached by a sliver of flesh.

"It bit me. There's something else in there, look at my finger. God save us, whatever is it? Fetch the priest, quickly." The serving girl hurried out of the room.

Tupas stared at the damaged finger, open mouthed and ashen-faced.

His spouse was fading away in front of him. Her grip on his hand loosened, but she found the spirit for one last blood-curdling scream as her cervix widened, and the thing emerged. The nurse screamed again, not at her bloody finger, but at the slimy red creature that slithered from between Maria's shaking legs.

The bald head looked almost human, but the red eyes and the open mouth, with rows of serrated teeth, was a macabre sight. Slime and blood streaked across the red scaly skin which wriggled out of the now unconscious woman. The thing had withered hands, like small talons emanating from its rounded shoulders. Below the neck the human skin gave way to a lizard-like covering. The narrowing body of the beast followed the head until it was out, lying coiled up between the woman's legs. Everyone was shocked by the apparition wriggling before them.

A quiet mewing came from the new-born baby girl in a cot by the bed. It caught the attention of the monster. Before anyone could intervene, it slid over to the cot, and without hesitation sank its pointed teeth into the flesh of its twin. As if carving off a slice of turkey, the beast tore off half a shoulder; the arm came with it. What was left of the baby cried no more.

Oliver, Tupas's sixteen-year-old son, rushed across the room. He'd just come home and heard screaming coming from the bedroom. He couldn't take in the bloody scene before him. He saw his mother lying open-eyed and lifeless on the bed and ran to her.

The monster mistook this for an attack and lunged at the boy. Oliver's reactions were quick. There was a surgical scalpel lying in the tray. In one swift move he embedded it in the fiend's throat. It spluttered; blood was running from its mouth. Oliver fell onto the beast with rage. He raised the short blade and stabbed again and again until beast's neck was in tatters. Then he lay back crying on the body of his dead mother.

Moments later the priest appeared. He was an elderly man who walked with a stick. He stood in the doorway open mouthed and instinctively clutched the silver crucifix around his neck. Tupas looked at him, helpless, and nearly out of his mind.

"What happened here? The girl told me, but I didn't understand her. What in the name of heaven is that?"

He spotted the mass of scales and blood on the bed. Tupas was on his knees sobbing. He couldn't accept what had happened - the monster, the death of his new daughter and his wife. He was in shock.

"What have you done, my son? Why has such evil visited you? This is the Devil's work."

The Rajah looked up at the Holy man. How did he know?

"Father, has someone told you who I am, do you know my past?"

The priest was a Filipino, so Tupas could confide in him.

"I know nothing about you, my son. I've seen some evil things in my career, and each time they result from someone incurring God's wrath by an evil, or unspeakable deed. What did you do to make God so angry?"

"Father, please believe me. I didn't mean to do it. He shouldn't have been there, then he wouldn't have been hurt, he should have left me alone."

"You better tell me the full story."

"Father, I'm so sorry. I'm the one that burned the new church in Cebu. I killed the young priest. It was an accident; he just wouldn't get out of my way. Before he died, he cursed me and my family for generations. What have I done, father? How can I make amends?"

"My son, I've heard of the burning, and the massacre. Your wickedness cannot be forgiven, now or ever. God will have revenge on you, and maybe on future generations."

***

The same priest buried the mother and the baby daughter. They threw the grisly remains of the monster on a bonfire.

Late in the evening the ashes were just smoldering, and no-one was around. A cloaked figure sneaked out from the shadows and reached into the ashes. It lifted the warm remains of the beast and sloped off with the ghastly remains in a sack.

Tupas did not attend the funerals. His complete breakdown confined him to his chamber, howling and screaming. He was inconsolable.

After five days he awoke, rose and dressed normally, then made his way to the church. There was no-one there, but the side door was, as always, open. He was carrying a flask which he put beside the altar. He bowed his head, kneeled and prayed.

"Holy Father, I've done you a great wrong. Words cannot say how miserable I am. Men have died at my hand in battle, but that poor young priest didn't deserve to die, not in your house. How can I put it right, Lord? Please let the suffering stop with me. I implore you not to inflict such pain on my son, and descendants. They've done nothing wrong."

He pulled the stopper from the canteen and poured the oily liquid over his head and shoulders. He took a tinderbox from his coat pocket and struck a flame.

"My soul is yours, Lord. Do with it as you will. I beseech you to spare others." He dropped the glowing taper onto his oil-soaked clothes. Blue and red flames flickered around the hem of his coat and pants. They crept upwards and along the seams. His naked feet were first to suffer the pain. The heat, the unbearable agony. He tried hard not to shout, but couldn't stifle his screams as the flames moved along his legs. He smelled his own burning flesh as the fire took hold. His hands were burning balls of flame and his head and face were soon engulfed.

"I'm sorry, Lord." The tortured man's last words were a whisper, his mouth was melting now. As life left him, he held up the small wooden cross he always wore around his neck. Collapsing forward, he could only gurgle now, and pray that death would come quickly.

CHAPTER THREE

MODERN TIMES

Modern day Cagayan de Oro is a very different place. The Spanish left two hundred years ago, and the island developed into a holiday getaway, with modern resorts and services. With its sandy beaches and waving coconut palms the region became a popular place for holidaymakers.

Over several generations the Constantinos grew rich and powerful; the chilling stories of olden times were now consigned to fables and used to frighten children into obedience.

Exotic golden beaches edged by lofty palms swaying in the balmy breeze fronted the Governor's estate. Many resorts, hotels and beaches attracted wealthy foreigners and locals. The family had buried its unholy secret. Modern generations believed it was just a legend and had never really happened.

One tranquil evening in the summer of nineteen ninety-seven there was much commotion in the palatial residence of the Governor. His wife Emily was expecting their first child. She was a strong woman and had carried well. She took to her bed during the morning. By the evening, the midwife and doctors came. The baby would be born that night.

In-keeping with the stature of the family the birth was a big affair. They were a land-owning political dynasty and ran the sprawling province. Juan Constantino was the provincial Governor. His two elder sons controlled his businesses including construction, tobacco plantations, mango and pineapple groves and rice fields which brought their legitimate income.

They earned their real riches, at least in recent times, from illegal gambling activities. Illegal betting was popular amongst the workers and townspeople – and controlled by the Governor himself. His stature and power prevented any interference in their Golden Goose from 'the Authorities.' He was the Authorities.

A typical hypocritical Philippino politician, he worshipped God on a Sunday and behaved in a most ungodly way during the week. However, he thought himself to be a good, devout man. To his warped sense of thinking, when he had someone killed, they deserved it; they were a lesser man than him. God told him so.

His high status meant that no-one dared to contradict him. Over time he'd come to believe that he never did anything wrong, and God would always bless whatever he did.

He paid regular weekly visits to Church. He wanted to show God his devotion. From his family pew he watched the lines of people waiting for confession. He had no need of that,

God protected his illegal gambling profits, his protection rackets etc. God allowed him to 'take care' of any problems. It was the same reasoning that convinced him he was not unfaithful to his wife if he didn't sleep with other women. Young boys were a different matter.

He was, in truth, an unlikeable man. The worst of the Constantinos for many generations.

***

Sweat beaded on her pale brow and her mouth gaped open. Emily was exhausted. Her labor had already lasted for hours. This was her third pregnancy, she'd expected it to be easier. Her discomfort was worse than for the other births. Something didn't feel right. She was in great pain, and such swelling, but she still didn't realize that the growing discomfort in her belly was only the dark beginning.

The two attending physicians were not concerned. They'd been in attendance for the previous births, with no problems. The younger doctor glanced over at the bed.

"Check the cervix, nurse. There should be some movement by now; it's been a long time."

The new, young, midwife checked between Emily's legs, then shook her head at the doctors before busying herself keeping the expectant mother comfortable.

There was an incessant tapping as the edges of the beaded lace curtains brushing against the wooden frames, yielding to the light breeze. A torrential thunderstorm had blown itself out only that morning. A quiet whirring came from fans set at the corners of the spacious room, each one directing a robust breeze onto the ornate wooden four poster bed set against the far wall.

Within minutes the midwife finished her examination and nodded at the two doctors.

"Eight centimeters. She's ready. It'll come now."

Three heads turned toward the bed as Emily let out a high-pitched scream and spread her legs as wide as possible. The scream intensified as the slimy head protruded. A small pink body, streaked with blood and fluid, slid through the stretched canal. Within a few moments the older of the two doctors was holding the newborn. He wiped the mucus from the mouth and nostrils, and smiled as it cleared its mouth.

First a quiet mew, and then a louder wail came from the healthy young baby cradled in his two hands. He held it in his outstretched arms as if presenting a bouquet.

"Ma'am, you have a healthy young girl. At last you have a daughter."

Emily's tired and sweaty face broke into a weak smile as she held her hands out to receive the precious bundle. Suddenly, the smile disappeared, and the blood drained from her face. Her eyes widened, and a scream returned to her lips even before she could hold her baby. She looked down at her stretched stomach. It was still moving.

"Oh, my God. There's something still there – I can feel it moving, wriggling. What is it? Get it out of me."

She beat the covers with clenched fists, crying out as she squirmed amid the damp sheets. The older doctor rushed to the bed and felt her undulating abdomen.

"There's a twin. There's another one. Quick help her." The nursemaid rushed back to Emily.

"I can see another head. This one's coming fast."

The two doctors leaned over and paid close attention as the mother writhed and the nurse reached forward to assist.

"The head's out now. Relax and push as much as you can."

Emily strained and arched her back, wincing in agony.

"Why is this time more painful? It feels strange...ugh..." She gave a final push.

"It's coming now. I can see the shoulders. Just one more big push. The body's.... oh my dear God.... Doctor – what the hell is that?"

The two doctors didn't reply. Their mouths were wide open, their faces ashen as they recoiled from the bed. The hellish, bloody twin was out now, laying wet and glistening with slime, on the sheets looking up at them. No one rushed to pick the monster up. The eyes looked up, appealing for love, for contact. It couldn't reach its arms up – there were just small stumpy limbs. More like a lizard's front legs.

It had no back legs, just a snake's body which tapered and coiled beneath the sinister head. When it stretched out, the greasy abomination was about four feet long. Slimy yellow scales reflected the light from the crystal chandelier above.

Writhing and twisting, the monstrosity cried out. It had a baby face and from the neck up might have been mistaken for a normal child, until it opened its mouth. No normal child is born with a full set of teeth, long, pointed ones.

The doctors were dumb struck, and more than a little afraid. The younger one spoke first.

"What should we do? Should we kill it? We shouldn't allow it to survive. This monster is an affront to God."

On the bed, Emily was sobbing. She wouldn't even let the midwife clean her bloody legs. She tried to pull away as the serpent/baby slithered beside her. The older man spoke.

"We can't kill it, the decision isn't ours. We'll wait 'til the Governor gets here. He can decide." He put his hand on his colleague's shoulder.

Governor Constantino was sat in his study next door waiting for news when the hysterical maid burst in. He couldn't believe what he was being told. He rushed into the room as the doctors finished their discussions. The midwife was on the bed comforting his wife. Both wept.

"Sir, we've never experienced anything like this before. What do you want us to do, sir?"

The younger doctor feared for his life. The Governor was unpredictable. He may take this out on the medics. Constantino ignored the whimpering doctor and focused on the scene on the bed. He addressed the midwife.

"Fetch the first born, the girl, she needs her mother's comfort. Quickly girl!"

He turned to the doctors, stern faced. And glanced at the writing beast.

"Get me a basket. And don't harm him. Do you understand? I want him cared for. Put him in a box and bring him to my chamber. If anything happens to him, I'll hold you responsible."

"But sir, you can't let such as thing live. It's ungodly."

The Governor eyed him without expression, he tolerated no dissent.

"I will excuse your impudence because of your youth, lad, but listen to me. If he dies, so do you. Is that clear?"

As the frightened man scurried away, the midwife returned with a tiny bundle in her arms. The newborn girl was screaming now. She placed it beside the still sobbing mother. Without a word to his distressed wife, the Governor strode out of the chamber.

He meant what he said to the young doctor, both the medics knew it. They found a basket and a soft blanket. It was small, and, despite its physical appearance, seemed friendly. It offered no resistance as they placed it in the basket, nestling down into the blanket.

The Governor locked himself in his office and sank to his knees – clasped hands held up in the air. Why had God chosen him? Was this God's revenge, and why had it taken so long to resurface?

"Lord. I've dreaded this day and hoped it might never come. I've led an obedient and worshipful life. I'll play my part Lord. Give me strength, please, to do your will."

CHAPTER FOUR

REAPPEARANCE

Earlier in the year, with the birth of their second child coming soon, the Governor and his wife had decided to remodel the old house. For hundreds of years the structure had withstood the wear and tear of generations. Some of the supporting walls needed to be taken down and repositioned.

After the builders put the necessary supports in place, they set about the dirty work with heavy lump hammers. To their surprise, inside one wall they uncovered a cavity; the men fetched a torch and peered inside.

"Sir, you better come over here. There's something strange inside."

The Governor was reading the morning newspaper in his study. He strode over to the large hole, covering his face against the dust and looked in. As his eyes became accustomed to the light, he saw something in the corner. He reached in and pulled out a dusty parchment, and a cloth sack. The book was an old leather-bound ledger.

He carried the strange objects over to his writing desk. After putting the bag down on one side he opened the ancient sheet. The writing was quaint, but he could just about understand it.

"I am Oliver Constantino, son of the late Rajah Tupas, now Constantino. If you've found this book, you're probably my descendant, a Constantino. You must read this to the end. I have written these words as a warning to future generations of our family.

My father was not an evil man, but he did some things which the Almighty God would not forgive. Many years ago he burned down a church and killed a priest, who cursed him and his descendants before he died, burning and in agony. That started the tragedies destined to befall us.

While I was still a boy, my mother died in childbirth, but not before giving birth to a monster, an abomination; it was God's punishment on my father. I killed the thing, but the tragedy caused him to take his own life, so I grew up an orphan. Thirty years on now, I have a family of my own. Thank God that my children are normal.

Many times I talked with the old priest who witnessed my mother's and sister's death and my killing of the beast. He made me promise to write this warning. I killed the monster that God had sent as punishment. The priest told me that God would keep sending it. If someone killed it, the beast would come again. He said the only way to rid the family of this infinite curse would be to let the abomination live. To care for the monster until its natural death, then the debt would be paid. That's the burden and cross our family must bear.

Please give this warning on to your children and tell them to pass it on. I give thanks every day God has spared me, but I believe a future generation will pay for his sins. If you don't believe my words, please look in the sack beside this book. God help us all. Oliver Constantino."

The Governor folded the parchment and eyed the dirty sackcloth bag. He opened the top, but was frightened to put his hand inside. Instead he emptied the contents onto his desk. The bones looked like those of a large lizard. Although they were scarce now, in olden times large monitor lizards, some as long as six feet, inhabited the nearby mountains.

He had seen skeletons like this before. Then he noticed the head and gasped with astonishment. It was the skull of a child, a human child, but with pointy, spiky teeth. He examined it closely. It was no trick, no lizard and boy joined together. It was genuine. The old man trembled as he placed the remains back in the bag.

He opened the large safe fixed into the wall and put the macabre article and the book inside. The strongbox had a key and a combination. He kept both very secret. The world would ever see what he had just seen and read. It would go with him to his grave.

***

The joyous bustling that had engulfed the house earlier in the day was gone. The sky darkened, as if in sympathy with the family and the ominous event. The corridors inside the mansion were quiet now. The Governor knew what he must do.

Bodyguards accompanied him everywhere. Men were always stationed outside the bedroom door. He beckoned them to follow him to his chamber. He exchanged a few whispered words with them out of the earshot of the doctors before closing the door.

The medics followed a few moments later. He dismissed them after they placed the basket on a side table.

He waited until he was alone, then approached the writhing thing. Without hesitating the Governor picked up the small bundle. He whispered, as he stroked the human-like head.

"I'll look after you, son. Don't worry, I'll keep you safe."

The little monster gazed up at him, and he smiled back. Then the reptile thing opened its mouth, showing its fang-like teeth and the doting father looked away. He called the doctors back into the room.

"Gentlemen, God has treated me well over the years. Now he has sent this child. It's a test of my faith. I must atone for the sins of my ancestors. It would be an affront to Him to do anything else. I will treat this boy as one of my own. Your work is finished now, you may leave. My men will pay you on the way out."

The Governor spoke to them without his eyes leaving the thing. They left without saying a word. Outside the door, the waiting guards fell in line behind them.

"Wait in your car, we'll bring the cash out to you. We have to see the Governor's cashier – it won't take long."

The air was cooler now as the doctors strode through the side entrance out into the forecourt. Pleasant scent of jasmine trees was on the still air. The small courtyard behind the kitchen had cobbled stones – a throwback to its Spanish origins. It contained just three vehicles. The large Humvee belonged to the Governor, as did the Ford expedition.

The dirty white old Camry belonging to the doctors was hidden away at the back in the shade of a large mango tree. They settled into their seats to wait for their money. The larger guard approached the driver's side while his partner walked up to the passenger window. In anticipation, the doctors opened the window to receive their pay.

The guards were holding the envelopes they expected. But the medics were not expecting the bullets that hit them simultaneously. These thugs were experienced. The first shots were fatal, but they pumped two more shots into each man to be sure.

They were trained assassins, they knew their job, there was no need to check. No-one was breathing inside the car. The doctor in the passenger seat laid back with his head to one side, as if sleeping. The driver was slumped forward with the wound to his right temple oozing dark blood which dripped onto the floor adding to the pool of blood and brains that slid down the door when his skull exploded. Blood and brain matter were splattered over the window. News of the evil that had occurred there that night would not get out. The Governor made sure of it

Disposing of bodies, and even cars, was not a problem in this rural area for such anyone who worked for such a powerful man. There were quarries, buildings and bridge foundations, deep fishponds, they had many choices – and Constantino never asked.

No-one dared to enter the master's bedroom. He was still holding his new son when he heard six shots ring out from the courtyard. Stroking the forehead of the now sleeping beast, he smiled and whispered.

"Sleep well, son. I'll do my duty; you won't have to fear anyone or anything."

There was no sign of the gender of the thing, but he knew it was a boy, God told him so.

The midwife tidied her mistress's room; he was doing her job with no real thought. Her mind was still trying to come to terms with recent events. Emily slept now. The nurse decided to leave and rest for a while.

She had her own room next to Emily's. As she approached her room the two returning bodyguards appeared. She said nothing. They were always around, but she never spoke to them. She feared them, with good reason. After opening the door, she turned, surprised to find the men close behind her. She stopped, but they did not. They pushed her into the small room. It was dark, the curtains were still closed; the bed took up most of the space, so it was easy for them to push her back onto it. Before she could shout the larger of the men covered her mouth. The other guard approached the struggling woman and lifted her skirt, revealing her lily-white legs. She clawed at his hand, unable to breathe.

"Hmm. Seems a shame to waste it." His friend nodded.

"Go ahead. We're going to kill her anyway."

The smiling man dropped his pants and lay on top of her, his strength and weight were too much for her; she lost consciousness as he entered her. As he repeatedly pushed, her body gave up the effort. She drew her last breath as he wiped himself on her skirts.

***

As Emily awoke the next morning, her husband sat on her bed, holding her hand. She glanced around anxiously. The baby girl dozed in a cot at the other side, safe. She squeezed his hand.

"What did you do with it?" Part of her wondered if the monstrous thing that slithered out of her womb the night before was just a nightmare.

"I set him up the spare room. He's sleeping. I put extra locks on the door. He can't get out, and no-one can get in."

A look of disbelief came over Emily's face.

"It's still alive? How could you let that thing live. It's evil. We must get rid of it. We can't keep it here. Why in God's name would you want to let it live?"

The Governor decided against explaining the book and the grisly skeleton to his wife, she wouldn't understand.

"Emily, it's a trial we have to bear. I'm sorry, but we must care for it. Don't worry, I'll see to it. You won't have to have anything to do with it."

She withdrew her hand from his. She would never hold his hand again.

At first the Governor tried to feed the thing on oats and thin porridge, but there was no response. It nibbled at some cooked chicken he brought, but with little enthusiasm. As an experiment he brought in some raw liver. The animal gulped it down with relish. From then on, the beast grew stronger on a diet of only fresh meat.

The Governors marriage to Emily had never been a close one. She'd put up with him and in return led a quiet, safe and prosperous life. They'd become more and more distant in the weeks since the birth. He displayed increasingly bizarre behavior, taking meals alone and spending time in the locked room that had become the monster's world. No one else would dare to enter, even if the door wasn't locked. He paid no attention to the rest of his family. Emily had called their daughter Sophia – the Governor showed no interest.

Emily somehow coped with living for three more years before falling from the highest balcony of the house onto the concrete floor. Constantino told himself it was an accident, but he knew the truth was she just didn't want to live anymore. He was just a little surprised to realize he didn't care that his wife was dead, or about his young daughter who was bewildered at the loss of her mom.

At three years old, Sophia was too young to understand that her mum had died, or to object when she was shipped off to stay with relatives. She'd hardly ever seen her father, neither of them missed the other after she left. They would never see each other again.

CHAPTER FIVE

THE INCIDENT

The incident five years later with the young kitchen maid changed everything. Paulo, the new chief cook came from a distant province and moved into the big house with his wife, Tamara, who joined the cleaning staff. He was a little too fond of alcohol; he hid bottles around the kitchen, and was far from faithful to his long suffering wife.

When the new girl, fresh from school took up her duties he decided he must have her. She avoided his increasingly bold advances for two weeks until one night he found her alone in the pantry and wouldn't take no for an answer. Roughly, he pushed her against the wall with his powerful hands over her mouth so she couldn't scream.

He pinned her hands behind her back, more concerned with lifting her skirt up at the front. Her left hand found a corkscrew at about the same time as his other hand had pushed her undergarment to the side. The stabbing pain in his side stopped his progress just in time. He relaxed his hold on her and she slipped away screaming.

As she ran down the corridor the door at the end opened and the master came out. In her blind panic she ran inside before the Governor could stop her. As usual the room was dimly lit and badly ventilated. The smell hit the poor girl as soon as she entered, but in her panic she kept on running.

I the darkness, he tripped over a feeding bowl on the floor and stunned herself as her chin struck the wooden boards. She awoke with a sharp pain in her neck. The smell was now overpowering and the fangs, now mature and several inches long were embedded in her throat. One had hit the artery and blood spurted out.

She struggled to scream but her mouth filled with blood. The gurgling was the last sound she made. The whole thing took less than ten seconds. The Governor watched all of this, but was too slow to help the poor girl. He closed the door and locked it.

He sat with his son throughout the night as the beast took its time to savor the feast, like a lion after a kill. The old man watched it gnaw through sinews and chew muscle.

He left the room in the early hours of the morning, a troubled man. He did not care about the girl's death. God had obviously wanted the boy to feast on her flesh, but this time there would be repercussions.

He'd feared that this would one day happen. Despite the tightest security, rumors of the 'monster child' at the big house abounded in the town.

The distraught parents of the girl didn't believe she'd run away, especially after the dismissed cook spread tales around locally. Eventually the Governor compensated the family and they kept quiet. The cook stopped spreading the rumors. He'd suddenly disappeared.

"Are you working late, Paulo?" They surprised the burly cook. He didn't expect to find anyone else in the kitchen at this hour, but the Governor's bodyguards went wherever they pleased. They answered only to him.

"Big party tonight. Lots of cleaning to do," he replied tersely.

"The Governor wants you to take some pork up to the room."

Paulo rolled his eyes. It wasn't the first time they'd asked him to deliver food up to that awful room, but he hated doing it.

The men followed him as he carried the bowl out of the kitchen and up the stairs. He knocked on the door. The old man usually answered and took the food. They never allowed him inside. As he knocked for a second time, he felt a hand on his shoulder.

"Hey, what are you doing?"

One man pushed him forward while the other unlocked the door. He dropped the dish on the floor and struggled with them, but in a few seconds he was forced into the room. They left him inside in the dark. As he struggled to open the locked door, the smell hit him. He turned, fearful of what he might see but needing to find out.

His eyes were not yet accustomed to the darkness, but he detected a slight movement halfway across the floor on his left. The slow undulations became clearer as the monster, now ten feet long and standing four feet high above its coiled body slithered towards him. Gradually his sight adjusted. He saw a red glint, no, two red glints side by side. His watering eyes came to focus on the ghoulish face surrounding the eyes and he shouted out.

"Oh God, no. Keep away."

The words seemed to excite the beast. It opened the wide mouth to show a gleaming row of sharp incisors. No one heard the terrified man's desperate cries. He backed away into a corner and slid down the wall, now weak at the knees. It approached him.

It did not rush, but it had a curiosity and certainly a hunger. The beady-eyed face rose up above his head. Serpent-like, the head tilted from side to side as it regarded its next meal with eager anticipation.

For just a moment Paolo hoped it would lose interest and move away, but that was not it's plan. He felt two razor sharp spikes sink into his cheeks either side of his nose. It fastened on and was twisting back and forth.

The pain was unimaginable as the teeth cut through flesh and sinew. In just five seconds the monster pulled away with a dripping nose between its teeth. Paolo put his hand up to touch the wet hole in the middle of his face before he fainted in agony. He lay on the floor, blood pulsing in gushes from the black hole where his nose used to be. Spluttering, he choked as blood poured down his windpipe, slowly filling his lungs and drowning him. The beast looked down on the man, slowly chewing the fleshy nose. After a few minutes his food stopped moving. He moved in to enjoy the body at his leisure.

CHAPTER SIX

THE MOVE

Tamara was in bed, wondering where her erratic husband might be. She wasn't worried, just angry. She'd warned him. If he kept up the drinking and womanizing, she'd leave him. She turned over to sleep, promising herself that she'd pack her bags tomorrow.

He never returned, and after a week she started to worry. In the town gossiping women spread ominous rumors about what might have happened to him, but Tamara thought he'd just run off with another woman. She gave up on him after a month.

Tamara, although no spring chicken, was very presentable for her age. After her husband's disappearance, she became withdrawn, spending her time out in the garden, or reading in her room. She could often be found in the kitchen late at night. She had nothing else to do.

It was midnight, and the house was quiet. She was used to the solitude, but this night she was roused from her reading by the large wooden door opening. The Governor came in for some meat and found her crying.

"What's wrong, Tamara? Is it Paolo? Are you still missing your husband?"

She turned, trying to conceal her tears and red face.

"No sir, it's not him. I'm better off without him, but I get lonely sometimes. The kitchen is peaceful at this time of night."

The Governor nodded in empathy. In the last few years his life had revolved around the 'boy'. He'd cut himself off from the world to attend to his charge – he often felt lonely as well.

He comforted her and put his arms around her as she nestled into him. His finger lifted her chin upwards. Neither of them had planned or expected this. The seduction was mutual and happened naturally. Her eyes closed as the old man kissed her.

They were both hungry for comfort. There was little foreplay, neither of them had any reason to wait. He laid her on the kitchen table with her legs apart and pounded into her for all he was worth. Their meetings became a regular occurrence.

***

The Governor realized things needed to change. His son chewed on the joints and offal now presented to him, but grew restless and irritable. He'd tasted fresh, live, human flesh – and liked it. More than liked, he craved it. He became withdrawn and listless. His father feared for his health.

The 'boy' could raise himself up high off the floor now on his coils, and was five meters long. The room was large, but was becoming too small now. There were no signs it would stop growing, but a plan was forming in the powerful man's mind.

The Constantinos had many business operations. Mostly to launder the money from the gambling and other criminal earnings, but they owned some legitimate profitmaking concerns. One of these was the Stonewell Construction Company. His sons ran this young but up and coming Property Company – and they ran it well.

They had two thriving malls now, and another one under construction – their biggest one yet - the flagship of the company. It was half-built and rising fast on a prime site in Makati, the business center in the capital city of the Philippines. It would bring the family national prestige, and help the Governor in his political ambitions. That used to be the plan, but nowadays the man was getting visibly older and less interested.

He summoned the architects to his house. They pored over plans laid out on the large mahogany table in the ornate study.

"Well, yes sir, maybe we can do this, but why would you want such a big space hidden inside with only secret entrances?"

"We've known each other for years Manny, I would've thought you'd know better than to ask me a question like that. I have many 'interests' and some of them need to be managed quietly – I'm sure you realize that? All I'm asking is for a quiet place that no-one knows about, but that I can get into discreetly when I want to. Surely you can do this?" He placed his arm around the portly man's shoulders.

"I want you to take personal charge of this – no passing the work to a junior. If people get to learn of this, the place will be no use to me, and neither will you! Am I making myself clear?"

"You are my friend, loud and clear. I'll have the plans ready for your approval in a week."

Manny knew better than to cross the Governor.

"We'll produce two sets of plans – one to get us through the regulations and another to actually build. We must pay off a few building inspectors, but nothing we haven't done before. Don't worry, sir. You can rely on me."

"I'm sure I can Manny, thank you."

The smile was back on the Governors face now and his arm back across Manny's broad shoulder as he guided him out of the office.

***

Building work in the city center is a slow and dirty business. Major projects of a similar size have taken three or four years to complete. Governor Constantino's flagship project opened just two years after building work began. Retail space was in demand in Manila, especially in the more sought-after areas. Famous international stores occupied ninety percent of the space at the opening. The other ten percent would not be far behind.

Near to the Mall site, a residential tower block of small one and two bedroom apartments sprouted up. Developers built it to cater to the City's growing young professionals and call center workers.

Angela Garcia moved into her new two bedroom home just a few months ago; her parents were due to arrive at any moment for their first visit. She scampered around to tidy the modest apartment. She was a simple girl, she'd been in the city for seven years now and her acting career was taking off.

Despite the temptations, she'd never dabbled in the sleazy world of drink, drugs and sex as so many bright, starry-eyed provincial girls did when they came to the city.

She wanted her parents to be proud of her. Angela came from a simple farming family in Mindanao. They were poor, her parents hadn't traveled to Manila before. For the past year or so she'd been able to send them money to ease their poverty – and for the ferry to Manila, then taxi to her apartment.

The sharp knock startled her. She panicked; they'd come early. She hadn't finished cleaning.

"It's open." She called out.

The door opened and a small round face peered timidly into the room.

"Come in, mom. Don't stay in the doorway. Where's dad?"

An even smaller, thin man followed his wife into the apartment. His face showed the weather-beaten signs of a lifetime of working hard in the fields. Angela watched them gaze around as if they were visiting a stately home, then sat her over-awed parents on the cream couch in the center of the lounge. After settling themselves, the old lady looked up at her daughter with pride.

"You've done well dear, we're so proud of you, aren't we dad?" She turned to her husband who nodded. Angela became a little tearful, but didn't show it.

"It's different living here, mom. People are busy. They don't have time for you like folks back home. I miss that, mom, but I'm doing ok."

"How's that boyfriend of yours? Do we get to meet him? You haven't told us much about him."

Angela was quiet, but her mother wouldn't give up.

"He's not married is he? You're not a rich politician's mistress, are you?"

Her daughter rolled her eyes.

"Of course not, mom. He's just busy with his career. I'll try to get him to come over."

Angela and Joel had not been getting on too well. Angela feared if her parents met him, they wouldn't like him. Her mom would certainly pick up on their problems. She picked up her keys from the coffee table.

"We need some milk. I'll just go to the seven eleven. Make yourselves at home. Take a nap on the bed, you must be drained." She nodded towards the spare room on the way out. As soon as the elevator opened out into the lobby she pressed a speed dial on her phone.

"Please come over, Joel. You said you'd try. They've come a long way, and they really want to meet you." She sighed as he replied.

"Sorry, babes. Something's come up. I'll try to get over later."

"It's not a lot to ask Joel. Don't you care about my family?"

She closed the phone before he could answer and crossed the busy road to the convenience store. Beyond the row of small shops, the mall towered above the office blocks. In the short time since moving in she'd seen it rise from deep foundations. She eagerly awaited the opening. It would change her life much more than she could ever imagine.

***

The day for the grand opening came, with an appearance by the vice president himself. The Governor did not appear. He had other things to attend to. In the province he still had preparations to make.

"Look General, it's simple. I just need an armored personnel carrier for one night. That's not too much to ask after all I've done for you. I don't even need any of your men – my best guys are ex-military, they'll drive." Constantino berated the unfortunate officer.

"That's part of the problem, sir. How can I explain letting you take one of our most expensive vehicles without our men to take care of it?"

"It's non-negotiable General, and it has to be tonight. You will do this for me General. I shouldn't have to remind you what I did for you when your son raped that girl in my province. I looked after you then – I'm calling in the favor now. You know, the rape charge can still be revived – it's only been three years."

The general was quiet, he knew he was beaten.

"Twenty four hours. I can't cover for any longer than that. Can you be sure it's back by then?"

"Of course, but we need it at six o'clock tonight."

"Ok. Get your men to come to the camp. One of my guys will drive it and park up in the nearby side street on the right. He'll leave the vehicle open with the keys in the ignition. Make sure they drive straight away; someone will notice if it's standing there for a long time."

"All right General, they'll be there to pick it up at six tonight and they return by six tomorrow night to the same place. Thanks for your help."

As the evening wore on, he waited impatiently at his gate. They should be back by now. He was about to call them when he saw the large dark green ex-US military vehicle coming down the road. It could carry twenty armed men. Tonight it would have just one passenger, and comfort was not an issue.

"Ok, lads, you know where to go."

The Governor followed the vehicle on foot as it trundled around the house to the rear. Over the years he learned to talk with the vile thing in the locked room. The 'boy' could made noises that sounded like "food', tired', 'thirsty', 'hungry', 'girl'. He struggled with the sounds – they were more like hisses. Also, 'Girl' now meant 'Food' so sometimes it became confusing.

Tonight, he had to get his son into the vehicle. Concepts like 'safety' were beyond their rudimentary conversations, but he hoped that 'food' and 'girl' may do the trick.

It may not communicate well, but it certainly had a sixth sense. The Governor knew there was something wrong as he entered the room. The beast usually came forward to greet him as it heard the key turn in the lock. Tonight it remained cowered above its coils in the corner, regarding its 'father' with suspicion and fear. Its reptilian senses could smell the apprehension.

He pulled a chair closer, and sat. Calmly he stroked the boy's head, as he did each time he visited. He often talked at length to his son and believed the thing understood most of what he said. This evening he hoped more than ever that his words would be understood. The 'boy' had never left the room before and didn't understand anything outside of the four walls. Even if it could know right from wrong, it couldn't know it was wrong to kill and eat the girl. It had no point of reference to any behavior. Everything was pure instinct, an animal reaction.

He understood this, and had no idea how it would react to an attempt to move it. His two most trusted aides would help him. They knew the dirty secret. They wouldn't run when they saw the monster.

He spoke in soft tones. He knew the thing could kill him if it got angry, but it had never shown any signs of aggression toward him. Killing the girl was not aggression, it was just hunger.

The Governor looked on his resting, trusting offspring.

"Come on, son. Time for you to move to a nicer home with more room. Do you understand? The nearly human face regarded him, but showed no emotion.

"You'll have more room, and no-one will trouble you. I'll still come to see you every day. You'll be safe."

There was still no reaction.

"You'll get lots of nice fresh food. You'll enjoy it, I promise."

He thought he saw a slight reaction, but couldn't be sure. He moved in and put his arm around the near-human shoulders and held it close.

"Come on, son. It's time to go now."

He guided the thing forwards. It slithered towards the door with the Governor gently but firmly moving it along. The old man chose the time purposely; the whole house was asleep.

It was just forty yards down the stairs and into the carrier; they parked it close to the back doors. Under his instructions, the men put a young calf in as an inducement, it seemed to work

The beast didn't resist as it slithered down and out into the fresh air. It was with its father and trusted him. As they reached the door it lifted its head sharply, catching the pungent scent of the bewildered young animal cowering in the vehicle. It didn't need to be guided. It slid inside of its own accord. The Governor gently closed the doors with relief.

He climbed into the front with the two aides. They pulled away, ignoring the cries of the young cow struggling in the back as its throat was being torn open.

They arrived at the secured shopping mall site in darkness, just in time. In an hour it would be daylight. The guards opened the gates as they approached. Without stopping, they quietly drove around to the delivery bays, to the Governors secret door to the side, he had a key. The two men got out of the vehicle and came behind to help him. The Governor stopped them.

"No, it's all right. Get back inside. I think things will go better if I do this on my own. He may not react well if he sees you."

He had to push it hard, but gradually the small corrugated metal door creaked open – it wasn't used much. "Come on, son – we're nearly there."

The thing was slithering along beside its father, who still had a hand on it for reassurance. He guided it through the narrow opening into the large, dark, goods hall. Its eyes opened wide as it looked around. It showed no fear, but kept close to Constantino.

The strange pair left the stock area and disappeared down an alley to the back and into a large store. The builders left an opening to enable the Governor to sneak his abhorrent secret into the warm space created especially for it.

Inside the purpose-built inner sanctum, the air changed, and the light was even more reduced.

Bare brick walls were painted black and the workmen had installed a false low ceiling to keep him warm and comfortable. There was bedding, and warm carpets, and in the corner, a pit for his food. The men had already brought in the remains of the calf, still dripping with blood. Next to the pit an open tap trickled water into a drain below, the monsters drinking water.

When the beast caught sight of the meat, it straight away slid across the floor and gnawed on the bone and tore the flesh. Blood still dripped down the face of the thing from its frenzied feast in the van, but instinct took over, and freshly killed food comforted it.

In the corner of the pit was a small door, about five feet high and four feet wide. It was closed with three metal fasteners. The Governor checked it with approval, it fitted perfectly.

He stayed for a while until it the boy was asleep, and then slipped back out of the small opening to the outside. He slid a wooden panel into place and wedged it shut.

A couple hours later the beast stirred. With blood still spattered down its face and neck, the beast explored its new home.

This other home was warm, it was dry, and it was more interesting than his previous room. Suddenly something sparkled on the wall and he noticed a shiny object fixed to the ceiling in the corner above his food pit.

It was a mirror; he knew what it was because there was a mirror in his room at the estate. This one was different. It was like a car rear view mirror, but much bigger. It puzzled him. He couldn't see himself, it was angled away. They fixed it above the door, out of his reach.

In the mirror he could see over the wall. There was a small cubicle with three solid sides and a curtain for the fourth wall.

After a while, it lost interest. Folding its coils under the larger head in the usual way, it settled down and fell asleep on the mattress in the corner.

The beast normally woke at dawn, but today it was exhausted from the activities of the previous night. The next day, it was still asleep at ten a.m. when the Governor arrived. He climbed quietly through the small hidden door and approached his son. He was worried to see his son so still, but as he approached he realized the thing was only sleeping.

He glanced around in the dim light. The walls were dark and unfinished. Cement oozed out between the bricks in uneven lumps. In some places pieces had fallen to the floor. He pulled up the nearest chair and stroked the matted hair.

Over the years he had developed affection for the beast. He no longer saw a vile monstrosity, but a loving child. The duty of care grew less onerous. He was happy that his boy was now in a more secure place, at least for now.

"You'll be safe here, my son. No one will disturb you. You'll never need to worry – I'll always take care of you. God sent you to me for a reason. I know it's my duty, whatever the cost."

The beast stirred, and saw its father was there and let out a contented purr.

CHAPTER SEVEN

CONCEALMENT

Finally, the grand opening came. The new mall was the place be, and to be seen. Television personalities, politicians, actors, everybody shopped there. It was trendy, and the best international fashion stores were there.

By nine thirty in the morning lines of shoppers stretched around the building waiting for doors to open at ten. As the mechanical shutters rose up the eager buyers flooded into the walkways and the shops. Within half an hour the young middle and upper classes of Manila filled the clothes stores and tried on the latest fashions.

Butterflys, a popular and growing fashion store, was based in London. They'd invested a lot of money in their first shop in Asia, here in the prestigious new mall. As soon as the glass doors opened, bright young shoppers poured into the store. Customers soon filled the changing cubicles with young ladies in various stages of undress.

Inside the monster's den, the Governor was the first to hear the noises, but the unusual sounds woke the sleeping serpent thing.

"Come, son. I want to show you something."

As the boy rose on its coils the doting father guided it across the room, past the pit with the remains of the pig, to the door with the mirror.

***

Mandy was a Manila girl through and through. Her job as a call center operator paid well, and she worked the night shift to get even better pay and bonuses. Laughing, she flashed her half month pay, ten thousand pesos, in front of her colleague and friend, Anna.

"Hey, look what I've got. Wanna help me spend it?"

The girls giggled as they waited for the down elevator. Their busy office was on the twenty-fifth floor of the prestigious AXA building in Makati. The night shift was just finishing. Ten minutes later they were in a taxi and on their way.

"Where are we going?" asked Anna.

"I'm taking you to the new mall. There's a dress in Butterflys I've been promising myself. I hope it's still there."

The sidewalks in the center of Makati, the central business district, were packed as usual but the girls pushed their way towards the mall. From a distance she could see the dress was still in the window. A low-cut red cocktail dress with black sequins sewn into the shoulder and ribbons cascading down. It was very classy. She was happy. Pausing outside the shop, Mandy turned to her friend,

"Wait, here, I need to try it on. I'll come and show you." Mandy disappeared into the mass of people inside the store. Fifteen minutes later Anna was wondering how much longer her friend would be, she needed rest, and wanted to go home to sleep.

***

It was four days since the boy ate. The Governor knew he must be ready for another feed. Father and son approached the 'feeding pit'. The snake/boys attention was drawn to the mirror above. He saw movement. The slim, nearly naked girl squirmed as she tried to squeeze into the tiny dress. It was halfway up her thigh when she heard a noise behind her. Before she could turn around the back wall slid sideways.

Mandy's surprise gave way to utter horror as a ghoulish dark head with wispy hair and piercing green eyes appeared through the gap. The nightmare vision transfixed her with an intense stare as it opened its mouth wide revealing needlepoint fangs as the lips peeled back in a maniacal grin.

In less than a second, deadly, scaly coils tightened around her neck. The poor girl had no time to react. She gurgled, but the intended scream could not escape her lips. She could not resist the power of the beast. Her legs and arms flailed in all directions, but her strength was depleting; no air was getting into her lungs.

The monster dragged the limp body back into his lair. There was little life left in the young girl by the time it reached the pit. The boy could take his time now. Under the watchful gaze of his father, it settled down to feed. Pointed incisors sank into the soft flesh of the neck and dark blood spurted and pulsed out as her heart worked to maintain the diminishing pressure.

The mangled mess that once was Mandy lay lifeless in the pit as the serpent chewed contentedly on the muscles and sinews of her neck. He glanced up as the senator slid the opening closed. The old man stared at the mangled corpse dispassionately. He did not care that the girl had died, only that they should not get found out. They would have to be careful from now on.

***

Anna was getting cross. Mandy could be selfish. She forced her way impatiently through the mass of girls into the shop. She was tall and could see over the heads of most of the people there, but couldn't find her friend anywhere.

She pushed through to the changing area and waited for a few minutes while girls came and went with a variety of tops and pants. Finally, she gave up and peeked into each cubicle. Mandy was not there, she stormed out of the shop fuming. Her so-called friend had not only held her up for no reason, but did not even have the decency to find her and tell her she was leaving. She would never go shopping with the thoughtless girl again. She couldn't know that at one time she was just ten yards from her friend's lifeless body.

Nobody noticed Mandy's disappearance for nearly a week. She was a popular girl. It was common for her to stay away from her boarding house for a few nights, so no-one missed her for a while. Finally, her anxious parents arrived from the province. They were concerned. Their daughter hadn't answered their calls for the last three days.

Anna was surprised that Mandy hadn't turned up for work, but thought little of it. It wasn't the first time, and it still pissed Anna that the girl ran out on her.

The parents were poor, so the police didn't make much effort. They talked to Anna but took it no further. They told the distraught parents she'd probably gone off with a man and would show up soon.

***

People noticed the Governor's strange behavior. He'd certainly by now lost part of his mind – but in other ways he could still reason well. He still visited the beast most days and brought a goat, a pig, sometimes a small cow – he always came at night when the area was deserted. Each time he brought a live animal to keep his son well fed, there would be problems if girls disappeared every few days.

The lock on the 'feeding hatch' held, so the beast could only use it when the senator allowed him. Sometimes it needed to feed on warm human flesh, and drink the blood, fresh from the pulsing arteries. He just had to make sure that no-one could ever discover their dreadful secret.

He arrived back in the Province around five in the morning. Dawn was rising over the distant hills. The bedroom was in darkness, but Tamara awoke. She usually rose early, and anyway, she'd grown to expect him to get home at this time.

Their relationship was an open secret within the household now, with Tamara taking advantage of her new 'position'. A few months ago she'd started sleeping in the Governor's bed. The rest of the staff didn't cross her.

"Come to bed. You must be tired. Let me make you some tea." She rose, but the old man protested.

"Don't get up. It's early yet – you can take more rest. I don't need a drink. I think I'll sleep for a while."

***

Six weeks later the beast woke as usual at dawn. A shaft of light from the small skylight window at the top of the wall pierced the gloom. He looked in his pit. The stinking carcass of a goat lay in pieces. It chewed unenthusiastically on half a skull and found a few strands of flesh to nibble on.

It knew when the store was about to open. It could hear the buzz of activity. The shop girls and cleaners prepared the shelves and stock for another busy day. He eyed the mirror. No activity yet, but it knew it wouldn't be long. The excitement and anticipation began to rise.

He'd been working on the lock his dad used to prevent him using the door. Overnight he'd worked out the screws. The lock and the screws lay on the floor now. He could open it on his own.

Soon, the girls would use the cubicle; this would keep him occupied most of the day. It settled down on its coils and watched, transfixed as young girls took their clothes off. He was, after all, part human.

Today was different, he was bored with stale animals now. He needed to feed again. There was something inside him that made him feel differently about the girls he saw. Some he liked, mostly the thin ones. Some he would not consider as prey – generally the older ones. Several girls came and went, but they were not the right ones.

After a wait of about ten minutes, she walked into his cubicle. Unlike many of the others, she didn't rush. She pulled the curtain back and slipped inside. She was short and slim; he watched her peel her jeans down to try on the cocktail dress hanging on the back of the door. His eyes followed her movements as she rose to take the dress from the peg. Now was the time.

She was facing the curtain and didn't hear the rear wall slide open. She'd just pulled the tight top over her head when she felt a gentle touch against her ankle. At first, she thought it was a rat, but before she could scream, the monster's tail had curled around both legs and pulled her backwards with great force.

She hit the ground before she had time to react, splitting her eye socket on the edge of the wooden chair as she went down. In seconds the limp body was pulled roughly back through the wall and the panel closed. The only trace left of the girl in the cubicle was her jeans hanging on the peg, and her white fashion pumps on the floor.

Unlike the first girl, this one didn't move, she was already dying from the head wound, which now bled profusely. The smell of the fresh blood excited him. He licked the wound and lapped at the sticky red liquid. The feast lasted longer this time; she may have been brain dead but her heart still tried to work.

Instinctively, he seemed to know where to bite and chew to get the juice flowing straight into his eager mouth. Her neck became an unrecognizable mess within seconds. By the time his father arrived at midnight the gory body had lost most of its flesh. Strips of muscle and sinews dangled from the bloody bones which lay in an unnatural heap in front of the sleeping monster.

The Governor brought a goat with him, a young kid. When he saw the bloody corpse he knew it wouldn't want the goat. The boy would sleep for hours after such a meal, so he quietly left, taking the goat. His son would not want feeding for a few days after today's meal.

***

After many days, Mandy had still not returned home. Anna read the Philippine Daily Star a few days later when a top right-hand corner article caught her eye.

'Young girl disappears into thin air' The text continued... 'We are getting reports that a teenage girl entered Butterflys two days ago, and has not been seen since. Her parents say they waited for her outside and insisted she had never left. Someone called the police, but despite an extensive search they found nothing.'

Someone stole the jeans the unfortunate girl left behind, and her shoes. Anna remembered her trip to the mall and a shiver went down her spine. What if Mandy hadn't run off? What if she too had just disappeared inside the store? She rang the newspaper.

An hour later she sat in the editor's office, offering up her story. Two days later the story appeared. Front page news this time.

'THE CURSE OF BUTTERFLYS – ANOTHER GIRL DISAPPEARS'

Just a few weeks after the unexplained disappearance of one beautiful girl in the upmarket fashion shop, Butterflys, another teenager disappeared. Her distraught parents swear she did not come out after going into the store to try on a dress for her school prom.

The editorial described other disappearances which may have nothing to do with the unfortunate store, or they might. Other newspapers picked up the story, photos of the crying mother went viral on Facebook and YouTube. Many people came to Butterflys not to buy clothes, but just to see the 'haunted' shop. Others stayed away out of fear.

Such stories and gossip are not unusual in the Philippines. The people are generally very superstitious.

After a few weeks, the interest faded and sales picked up. Celebrities patronized the store again.

The Governor fixed a sturdier lock, and kept his son well fed with live animals to curb his cravings. It had been six weeks now and it hadn't fed on human flesh again in that time. The old man thought that maybe he should take away the mirror and seal up the door, but he waited a while longer.

CHAPTER EIGHT

NEW BEGINNINGS

Angela Garcia didn't hold with the 'fairy stories' about the mall, being a practical girl. Her parents were home in the province now, happy that their daughter was safe and doing well, but with many misgivings about her boyfriend. She'd never stopped shopping at Butterflys. All the assistants knew her - she usually went about once a week. Her star was rising. She had a good income now, and a lot of media attention. Bodyguards always went with her.

Each time she had visited the store a pair of piercing green eyes followed her every move in the dressing room. She might have paid more attention to the rumors had she known.

The thing became transfixed with her, and now studied every inch of her beautiful body. These images circled his brain and he now recognized her voice and rushed to the mirror whenever she came to his cubicle.

He'd watched his father fix a new bigger lock, but every night since then he'd worked it a little, it was nearly ready to come off. He left it in place so his dad would not realize what he'd done.

Conflict was an emotion he hadn't known before. Why was he fascinated with her? Did he want to eat her? He didn't like the idea that if he ate her, he wouldn't be able to watch her again in the cubicle. This confused him. But he wanted to see her, to touch her.

Angela was in a hurry today. She just had an hour before her lunch date to buy a nice evening dress for the party tonight. Her guards didn't need telling. They took up their station on either side of the shop entrance looking like bouncers at a night club – and waited.

Within ten seconds of her entering the cubicle the boy was at the mirror watching intently as she disrobed. He had to see her; he had to meet her. Carefully, he removed the lock from the door.

As usual, he waited until she faced away from the wall and quietly slipped the panel aside. Loud music covered the slight noises he made. His coils wound around her waist in a second and pulled her off her feet and through the gap before she realized what was happening. He pulled her to the ground, but this time he was gentle. She recovered her senses and turned to face her captor.

She never thought she might ever see anything like the horror that faced her now. Her eyes adjusted to the light and she saw the shiny, scaly tail and coils. Her gaze moved up to the vestigial arms with the clawed hands hanging from human-like shoulders. The long-haired head that sat atop the coils looked friendly and normal - until it smiled. The pointed fangs that protruded downwards from the jaws were terrifying. She tried to scream, but her mind gave up. She fainted.

As she came round the stench hit her. The sickening odor of decaying flesh pervaded the thick, humid atmosphere. Within seconds she remembered where she was. She panicked, but she seemed ok.

She wasn't being molested or eaten. In fact, her captor sat on its coils about ten feet away, regarding her intently with what seemed like friendliness. It didn't seem as if he was about to pounce on her, in fact it had a benevolent, quizzical expression, and its mouth was shut now, hiding the fangs.

She couldn't have been out long. The panel where the beast dragged her through was now closed, but in the mirror above she could see her clothes still hanging up in the empty cubicle.

She inched towards the door, watching carefully for any reaction from her captor. He saw her movement and didn't react. He didn't wish to kill her, he wanted her to live, to breathe, to stay with him... but she wanted to leave... What should he do?

She looked frightened. A sense inside him told him that if he tried to stop her, or move towards her, she would scream. Then he'd have to move quickly to silence her forever, but he didn't want to kill her, not this one. He wished to be her friend, but he had enough intelligence to realize that this would never be.

The monster stayed motionless as she eased towards the wall, growing more confident as she neared the panel. She pulled herself towards the opening and slid the door open, watching closely for any movement from the thing. It remained motionless, but continued to fix her with a beady stare.

Something inside told him, as he watched her disappear through the hole, that nothing would be the same now. The snake approached the opening and closed it behind her.

From the inside of the cubicle no trace remained of the entrance to his lair.

She was on the floor, inside the changing room, petrified with fear. A slithering noise came from behind the wall reminding her of the ordeal. Finally, she found the wit to scream. The high-pitched trill resounded in the shop and outside into the mall. Shoppers and staff alike stopped what they were doing and looked around for the source of the noise.

In the shop security guards rushed into the cubicle to find a near naked hysterical girl babbling and crying uncontrollably. A counter assistant brought in a robe and put it round her shoulders.

"Get me out of here." She screamed.

"Call the police. It's a monster. It nearly killed me."

Her own guards arrived and took charge.

"Come on Miss, we'll get you away. We don't want you here when the police come." She nodded through her tears.

They guided her through the mall and out into the parking area.

The wide-open space, with lots of people around seemed to calm her and give her some comfort. She struggled to make sense of what had just happened. Did it really happen? Could it be just a hallucination? What should she do?

They bustled her into the car. Luckily it had tinted windows. With tires screeching they sped off into the Manila traffic.

She had a reputation for common sense and good behavior, unlike her contemporary celebrities – she didn't want to damage that. But she couldn't just do nothing – not after what she'd gone through.

She only wanted one person, Joel. Within thirty minutes she burst into his office, sobbing. He put his arm around her shoulder.

"Come on sweetie, this isn't like you. You're normally so level-headed. Have you been taking drugs or something?"

Angela was affronted, and stared at him.

"How can you say such a thing? You know I've never done anything like that." Joel didn't press it.

"Well, I had to ask. You're not making any sense. You rush in talking of monsters and such. What d'you expect me to think?"

"If you don't believe me, come back to the store with me and see for yourself."

"Ok, I will. The Governor who owns the building is my friend. Perhaps he's there. We can meet him in the mall. I'm sure he can put your mind at rest. Let me call him."

Joel had met Constantino at several political functions. They were more acquaintances than friends, but they belonged to the same political party and Joel was a rising star in the entertainment industry.

"Hello, sir. How are you? – It's Joel Valencia. Remember me?"

"Oh, yes Joel, of course I remember you. How can I help you?"

"Sir, I have a strange request. Angela was in your mall earlier today, in Butterflys. She had a weird experience. She says some sort of snake monster attacked her." The Governor paused, and then chuckled.

"Are you serious, Joel? Is this a joke? Is it a publicity stunt? I don't mind going along with it if it doesn't affect me or my business. I'm very protective of my reputation you know."

Joel persisted.

"It's not a joke, I'm afraid, sir. She's really upset. We don't wish to cause any trouble, but she won't let the matter rest. Can we come and see you? We can have a good look around the store and the stockrooms – can set her mind at ease? Perhaps we can open up the back of the changing rooms just to prove to her there's nothing there?"

The Governor felt the unease well up inside.

"No. I will not allow you to poke around my store on the whim of a delirious girl. You stay away from here. Don't bother me again… or you'll regret it."

The phone went dead before Joel could respond. Angela was sat next to him, she hadn't heard every word, but certainly understood the gist of the conversation – she could tell by the look on Joel's face.

"If he won't take me seriously, I'll find someone who will. How dare he? I'll show him!" She stood up and flounced away.

"Sweetie, wait, calm down. Let's think this through before doing something we may regret."

The door slammed the door behind her before he'd finished speaking. She didn't wait, she didn't want to think it through. She acted straight away – not caring if she may regret anything.

***

The incident troubled the Governor as he drove home that night. How much longer could he keep this up? The truth must come out eventually, then his whole life, his business, his family, would all collapse around him.

He climbed quietly into bed beside Tamara, already asleep, careful not to wake her. She needed more sleep nowadays, and she found it more difficult to move around. Because of her pregnancy she only did lighter duties now. The old man guessed she must be close to term, her tummy was big, but he didn't take much notice of these things anymore. He had deeper, darker things on his mind.

The following mornings newspaper headlines did nothing to ease his concerns.

'FAMOUS ACTRESS MOLESTED AT MALL BY MONSTER. MALL OWNER REFUSES TO INVESTIGATE'

It was certainly the most exciting headline the Philippine Star had published for many years. The editor smiled. Sales would be good today. He made the distressed actress promise to go to the police – he thought of several follow up stories, they would be sensational and exclusive to him. The fat brown envelope he'd passed to the sobbing girl the previous evening proved a good investment.

The next day, Joel took Angela to see a police inspector friend. He was happy to support his girlfriend now, she'd shared the newspaper money with him. As they left their apartment block in the upmarket Rockwell complex Joel's phone rang, Governor Constantino spoke first.

"Look Joel, I'm really sorry about yesterday – you caught me at a bad time. Can you come over? Angela's a sweet girl. I don't want her upset. I want to reassure her."

"Well, ok, sir, if you're sure. We'll be round in a couple of hours."

"Who was that Joel?" Asked Angela.

"Governor Constantino. He wants to see us. He wants to make it up to you, he says. What d'you want to do?"

"Well, there's no harm in seeing what he has to say. Let's go?"

To their surprise, the old man waited by the side of the entrance looking out for them with two of his aides.

"Hello Joel, Angela, please come in. Come on up to my office." He was being very friendly.

The Governor shepherded them through the store to his private office. The secretary brought in fresh coffee and sat them down around a coffee table. The worried frown hadn't left his face since they arrived. Joel took the initiative.

"We're sorry to bother you sir, You're a very busy man. It's just that Angela thought she saw something when she was here a while ago."

"And what was that?"

The Governor did not look up as he asked the question. Joel stared at Angela, urging her to speak.

"I didn't 'think' I saw it. I DID see it! A bloody great snake, or a monster or something hiding in this building. Whatever it is, it's not natural. It grabbed me – I only just got away with my life."

Joel smiled, embarrassed.

"I'm sorry, Governor. She gets emotional. Obviously, there're no monsters here. She gets hot-headed I'm afraid."

Angela grew red with anger. She'd had enough of Joel's lack of support, in everything.

"Joel, how dare you! I thought you'd help me?" She turned to the Governor.

"It's there. I KNOW. It nearly ate me! Come with me. Let me show you the shop, we'll go through the hole in the wall – you'll see, you'll see what a monstrosity you've got there – maybe there are more of them. You've got to do something! Come on, I'll show you."

Constantino made no attempt to move, or to look at either of them.

"I'm sorry, Angela. I'm really sorry."

He didn't look at the two young people. His face seemed drawn, he looked old and frail. This was not the powerful, confident man that Joel knew. Joel wondered what could have happened to him in a few short years. Constantino's apology calmed the distressed girl.

"We don't wish to make trouble, sir. I only spoke to the papers yesterday because you wouldn't see us." The old man smiled, just a little.

"Thank you, my dear. I understand, and I apologize again for yesterday. Look, I wasn't thinking right. Perhaps I haven't been thinking right for quite a while."

The Governor was lost in a world of his own, but he snapped out of it.

"Angela, I must try to make amends, and preserve some dignity – not for me, but at least for my family. Please, can I ask you to withdraw the statements you made to the press yesterday. We don't need to inspect the shop. I accept there may be some truth in what you say you saw, but I don't want the world to believe such things. Can you help me, dear?

He had been quiet up 'til now, but Joel decided he should join in. He saw an opportunity.

"That's all very well Governor, but Angela's had a terrible shock, she can hardly stop crying. She's going to need a lot of therapy, and there's the damage to her reputation to think of."

Despite his fragile mind, the old man understood where this was going and he had no stomach for bartering over the matter, but he was liking Joel less and less and addressed the girl directly.

"If you'll retract the statement my dear, I'll give you enough to leave the country and live in luxury until this dies down. I can afford to be very generous."

Joel opened his mouth, but the Governor got in first.

"Don't worry Joel. I'll pay enough for you as well. I won't haggle. We'll write out a short agreement here and now and I'll write Angela a check for two million pesos."

Even Joel had nothing to say now. They sat silently as the man took his pen and his check book out. The old man looked up at Angela.

"My dear, very little matters now, except my reputation. I don't want my family to suffer for my … indulgences. Look, I've got a friend at CBS news, he'll interview you. That'll help to put the matter right. The quicker we do that, the less damage will be done."

Angela recorded the interview later that afternoon, with Gavin Costa, a popular tv show host. They aired it at eight o'clock the following day – prime time morning TV.

Angela took a rest from her packing to watch. The experienced newscaster addressed the camera.

"Well, folks, we have a strange turn of events now. Only two days ago a national newspaper carried a story about a monster loose in the newest and smartest mall in Manila. The report came from up and coming actress, Angela Garcia. She claimed a monstrous snake man had attacked her in a changing cubicle at the mall. Angela is in our studio now. She says the newspaper exaggerated her story, and that she overreacted and panicked because of stress and overwork. She's come here today to put her side of the story. Angela, tell us a little background. You visited the shop, didn't you?"

"Thanks, Gavin. Yes, I did visit the store. I often go. It's a wonderful store, and I'll go again."

"Yes, but you told the newspaper you had been attacked, didn't you?"

"Well, that's not strictly true, Gavin. I was never attacked or hurt. It felt like something behind the changing cubicle brushed against me, I panicked. Please remember, I've been working hard recently, keeping myself going with coffee and pills. They affected me – I wasn't well in myself."

"Are you saying now that you DIDN'T see a monster?"

Angela laughed.

"Gavin, we're both adults. There are no such things as monsters. I was stressed and panicky.

Perhaps I was hallucinating a little bit. As I look back on it, I feel foolish, but I hope everyone will understand the stress I've been under. I'm sorry. I never meant to cause a fuss."

"You said you visited the mall and met with the owner. How did he reassure you that all was okay? Was he angry at what you had said earlier?"

"No, he is a real gentleman, very understanding. He took me around. It's a great store and I'm sure there are no monsters now." She smiled.

"A lot of our viewers will find your complete change of mind in twenty-four hours very strange, Angela. How do you explain it?"

"Gavin. Your viewers understand me. I'm not a stupid, hot headed attention seeking bimbo. I got a degree before I started acting. They'll understand the stresses of being a celebrity and of over-working and I'm sure they'll see that I need to go away to recuperate."

"Ok, well. Thank you for coming in to give us your story, our viewers wish you well. Get well soon, Angela."

Angela smiled as she switched off the television. She was pleased with her performance. It would help her career. She just had one more thing to do before she left for the airport.

***

Joel was running late, but he still had plenty of time. Angela said the plane left at noon. He rushed up the stairs and let himself into her apartment.

"Hi babe, are you ready? We don't want to be late. Did you bank the check? I need some cash."

He suddenly realized the place seemed quiet and Angela did not reply. His eyes focused and he looked around. There was a white envelope on the coffee table with his name on it, he had an ominous feeling as he ripped it open.

"Joel, This will come as a surprise to you, but I'm going to America without you. You've been living off me for too long, and demanding half of the two million pesos yesterday was the last straw. You won't get a penny more from me for doing nothing and taking me for granted. Please don't follow or find me. It's over. Try working for a living. Goodbye, Angela."

Joel screwed it up and stormed out of the apartment.

The Governor was having a good day. He watched Angela's interview and on the whole he was pleased. The girl had kept her word.

***

Back in the province, Tamara would give birth at any time. He'd shown little interest in Tamara or the pregnancy, which was fine with her. She didn't particularly want him around. The baby would be her meal ticket for life. That was all she wanted.

***

The editor of the Philippine Star thumped his desk in anger. Early in the evening someone had brought him the late edition of his rival newspaper. The headline didn't please him.

'SNAKE MONSTER AT MALL – THE MYSTERY CONTINUES. ACTRESS WITHDRAWS HER CLAIM.' In bold caps - across the top of the front page.

He'd paid the girl a lot of money, and she'd reneged on their deal. Well, he wasn't a good loser and he would not let it go. He rehashed all the old stories and rumors he could find. He contacted a couple of the 'nut jobs' who'd previously come to him with crazy stories about the mall. He'd make sure he got even. In the final paragraph he hinted at a cover up and urged the authorities to investigate.

The Governor sat with his head in his hands. His phone rang. He was startled because usually his phone never rang. It was reporters. His private secretary knocked and came in.

"Sir, sorry to bother you. The paparazzi and photographers are waiting at the exits. I've told security not to let them up to this floor, but you will have difficulty leaving tonight."

He nodded and thanked her. After she'd gone he sighed and poured himself a whisky, then sat back in his leather swivel chair. He'd always thought he may have to face this day, but hoped to put it off for a while.

The loud beeping of the internal phone jolted him. He pressed the button. "Yes."

"Sorry, sir. It's Protacio, security chief. We've had a call from the police. They want to come and check out the whole structure. They say if we won't let them in they'll get a warrant."

Constantino sighed.

"Tell them there's no need for a warrant. We'll co-operate with them." He looked at his watch. It was eight o'clock.

"The mall will be closed in an hour. I'll meet them here at eight tomorrow morning. They can have access to everything."

"Ok, sir. Will do."

The Governors demeanor was solemn now, but serene. He remained in his chair finishing several large glasses of whiskey while thinking of his family, his business, his reputation. There was nothing left, he'd let it go in his obsession with his one deformed son. He'd done his duty, he'd looked after the boy, and where had it got him? Where was the higher purpose in what his actions? Maybe it hadn't been a test from God, or if it had been, maybe he'd failed.

Opening another bottle, he poured himself half a glass. How many glasses had he had? He couldn't remember. The alcohol was having an effect. He started to cry, and prayed to his God to forgive him.

By midnight there would be no one left in the store. He'd always kept a loaded pistol in his desk drawer. In twenty years he'd never needed to use it, until now.

He threw his whiskey tumbler against the wall. It was crystal and shattered into many pieces, with the alcohol forming a dark stain as it trickled down the expensive wallpaper. Why had God made him go through this?

Well, he didn't care. This was God's fault. But he'd show God.

Over the years he'd tried to love the monster. He'd had an unshakeable belief it was God's will he should bear this thing, and there would be a purpose to it, but what had it been for?

He would lose everything because of that belief, and he would go to Hell now, he had no doubt of that, and he didn't care anymore.

On his way to the back of Butterflys store he picked up a large shopping trolley and filled it with as much lighting fluid from the barbecue department as he could. It wouldn't spread as fast as gasoline, but it would do the job. By the time anyone realized what was happening, nothing could stop it.

The boy woke at the noise of the shopping trolley clattering over the concrete floor. The old man left the trolley a few feet away from the beast and walked over. He sat in his chair and rested its head in his lap as he'd done every time he visited. He stroked the boy's matted greasy hair and when he was asleep he eased the boys head back over the shiny coils.

He watched the sleeping thing for a few moments. Then he quietly pulled the weapon from his back pocket. His hand was shaking. He'd never learned to use it, it felt clumsy, but he was resolute. The old man steadied his gun hand with the other and put the gun closer. The barrel pointed straight at the center of the head as he squeezed the trigger.

The bang reverberated around the cavernous storeroom. The small hole in its forehead oozed with a pink mix of blood and cerebral fluid. A large red blob seeped from behind as its brains squeezed out of the large crack in the back of his head. A third of its cranium had exploded outward as the bullet traveled through and shattered its skull. A feint mew escaped from the thing's mouth as air gurgled from his throat for the last time. The tail thrashed up and down, the throes of death would last a few minutes.

Just for a few seconds the old man stared, relieved that it was over. He regarded the bleeding, slimy mess that used to be his son dispassionately now. There was still more work to do, no point waiting any longer.

One after the other the Governor opened the cans of accelerant and poured them over the beast, over the walls and the door, over himself, over anything that would burn. He wanted no recognizable trace left.

Finally, he sat with the remains. He felt lightheaded and disoriented with the whiskey and the gasoline fumes. He lit a match, and watched as it fell onto the boy. When he was sure the fire had taken hold, he raised the gun to his head, but his hands were wet with fluid and the weapon slipped from his grasp. He tried to go over to retrieve it, but the flames caught his clothes and soon covered his legs and arms. The pain started as the melting fabric caused the skin of his calves to blister. It rose quickly as the unforgiving fire found more weak spots of soft skin and sinew it could sear and melt.

He collapsed to the floor before he could reach the gun, but his screams continued until the flames engulfed him and there was no more breath. By the time the local fire crews were alerted, the inferno was out of control, there was little they could do except watch the inferno take its course.

There was a lot of timber framing in the building. The fire gutted the main structure. The builders had cut many corners. Cheap concrete crumbled and low-grade steel melted in the intense heat. When the sun rose, smoke filled the air all around and the walls were collapsing. The once impressive building was unsafe, it would soon become derelict.

***

In the Province, Tamara lay on her bed sobbing. The sheets were soaked with birth waters and blood. She hadn't expected it to come so soon.

They had tried to call the Governor since just before midnight but he didn't reply. Two servant girls attended the birth. The new young doctor had been sent for but hadn't yet arrived.

When the medic finally got there the scene of devastation was unbelievable. In between sobbing, Tamara was breathless, he listened to her chest and frowned. Her heart was giving out, she would not last the night. Something must have gone very wrong with the birth.

"It's a monster, doctor. I can't believe what just came out of me."

The wide glass doors were open, he noticed a slight trail of blood leading from the bed out into the yard and the bushes beyond.

"What the Hell happened here?"

He addressed the two frightened girls, staring at each one of them in turn.

"It's the work of the devil, sir. It must be. I'll not stay in this house a moment longer. God have mercy on us all." The eldest girl was nearly hysterical.

They ran out of the room to pack their bags. Tamara was now wide-eyed and gasping for breath. All the doctor could think to do was to hold her hand. Within minutes her shallow breathing stopped altogether.

***

The fence dividing the garden from the overgrown hillside was badly maintained, with many gaps and holes. Venturing out into the world. the Governor's new-born child opened its eyes to see the morning light for the first time. It was hungry. It could smell a rat nearby.

ABOUT THE AUTHOR

Arthur Crandon lives and writes in South East Asia, which is far from his birthplace – the South West of England. A former lawyer, he writes thriller novels – usually of a dark nature, and although fictional, they are always based on some elements of facts and true events.

If you want to follow his progress, visit his website: www.arthurcrandon.com

Or join his followers to get regular updates, news and offers

You can follow him on twitter: @arthurcrandon and friend/like him on Facebook:

facebook.com/arthurcrandonauthor.

And subscribe to his YouTube channel: Deadly Election

If you enjoyed BLOODLINE CURSE you would enjoy his first novel DEADLY ELECTION. It's about murder. intrigue, deceit and politics in the Philippines – it is a gritty and gripping read with many positive reviews. All Arthur's books are available from your favorite online bookstore.

You can get it at a discounted price here: Smarturl.it/DEADLY

His next book- PARRIS ISLAND HOTEL - will be released shortly

If you liked the book, please leave a review online, and to contact the author, you can email him at: ac@arthurcrandon.com

Printed in Great Britain
by Amazon

35241336R00059